Because I am the Only Child

from The Only Child Project Series

ISBN-13: 978-1502817624
ISBN-10: 1502817624

Published by Franklin Regal Pty Ltd, Canbcrra, Australia.

On behalf of
The Only Child Project
http://www.onlychildproject.com

I have lots of people in my family who **LOVE** ME A LOT.

Grandparents, aunts, uncles, & even a spuffle named Spot.

I'm always very busy,
with lots to do each day.
And I have lots of friends
with whom
I like to play.

But sometimes
it makes me
feel sad,
or little bit left out,

when I see
other families

with lots of kids about.

They have parties, wooly ball games,
& concerts to sing.

Siblings
PLAY with each other,
& help do the chores.
They have FUN together
& LIFE is never a BORE!

My friend Marty just can't understand how I feel.
He has forty-three brothers and sisters, and a pet rockateal!

"You don't know how lucky you are!" he finally said to me.
"If you hate folding your socks, try folding forty-three!

"I hadn't thought of that!" I said and so began to think.
Maybe being an only child doesn't really stink.
I'd been feeling sad, like a cloud blocking the sun.

But maybe I was lucky to be the only one.

So I thought about my **LIFE** & all that was fine.
I have my very own room,
where everything is mine.
I get to pick the place for every toy on my shelf,

ALL ABOUT ME!
SHELF

FIRST PLACE
FIRST PLACE
FIRST PLACE

& SEE
ALL
THOSE
TROPHIES?

I WON
THEM
ALL
MYSELF!

The pictures on our wall **all** show my smiling face.

When I want to use the mallmasher, I don't have to race.

If I need help with my homework, I don't have to wait my turn. Mom & Dad will always be there to sit and help me learn.

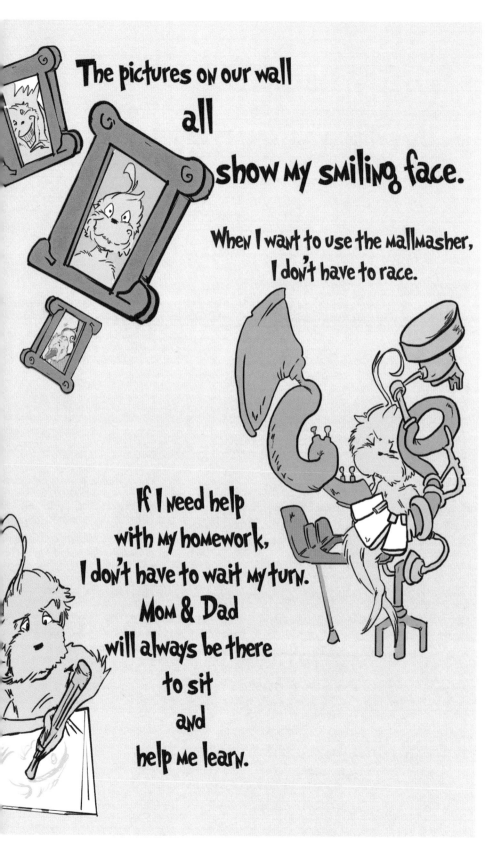

When we drive in
the wheelrambler,
it feels so great.

I can pick any seat I want,
&
don't get stuck in one I hate.

I get to choose
the spot
where we'll picnic

in the sun

&

I don't have to wait
for siblings,
because

I'm the

only one.

When Mom needs help in the kitchen,
I get to
lick the spoon
&
I get to shine the bell
when she cleans
the whirlafoon.

When it's time for **dessert,**

I get to eat the last slice. **And** when I need **Dad's** **attention,** I don't have to ask twice.

When I'm watching the view-a-vision,
I get to pick the show.

No one
changes the channel
or turns
the volume down too low.

When we sit on the slouchy puff,
I get the best seat.
When we go
to the Munch-a-Bunch,
I get to
choose
the
treat.

When Dad
is giving hugs,
I'M the first one in line
& when Mom
gives kisses,
every
smooch

is

mine.

Mom & POP market

XOXO

One day
I asked my parents a question
ON MY MIND.
I knew I could ask them anything,
on subjects of every kind.
My hands felt sweaty
&
My heart was beating wild,
&
I asked them
" Are you **happy**
to have
just

ONE child?

MOM

sat me on her lap,

with a **smile** on her face
& Dad wrapped his arms
around us in a loving
embrace.
"Of course
we are glad"
Mom explained to me.
"We'd never trade
our one child
to have
forty-three."

"We don't need any more children."
Dad looked me in the eyes.

"The day that we had you,
we knew we'd won the prize!

I thought about my life,

both the **good** and the bad.

And
I gave a big hug
to both
My Mom
&
My Dad.

I knew they were right,
our family is the perfect size.
It just took a little time for me to realize.
Now I can say I'm glad,
that I'm their only son.
&
I know they think I'm the best,

because

I'm the only one.

Made in the USA
Lexington, KY
03 April 2015